FULL OF LOVE

SHANI T. NIGHT

Intentionally Positive

Live to inspire the next generation.

— Shani T. Night

Paperback ISBN: 978-1-953364-47-0

Copyright © 2023 Shani T. Night.

All rights reserved.
No part of this publication may be reproduced, distributed, or transmitted in
any form or by any means, including photocopying, recording, or other
electronic or mechanical methods, without the prior written permission of the publisher, except in the case of brief quotations embodied in critical reviews and certain other noncommercial uses permitted by copyright law. For permission requests, write to the publisher, addressed "Attention: Permissions Coordinator," at the address below.

Infinite Generations
137 National Plaza, STE 300
National Harbor, MD 20745

Printed in the United States of America

First Printing, 2023

Art by Canva
Cover Design by: I Howard

Positive Media, Happy Life
www.InfiniteGenerations.com

INFINITE GENERATIONS PUBLISHING

WRITTEN BY SHANI T. NIGHT

Special Thanks to my family for their love and support.

You are the best!

FULL OF LOVE

The car is full of love.

We care for our bicycles with love.

When we travel, we travel with love.

Valentine's Day, you can bring home love.

When the fire truck arrives to put the fire out, it's full of love.

When the mail carrier delivers your mail, it's with love.

When birds sing, they sing with love.

When your grandparents visit, they arrive with love.

The truck is full of love.

A flower grows with love.

There are all kinds of love.

Teddy Bear love.

Animal love.

There's love in a hug.

There's puppy love.

Penguin love.

Elephant love.

There are love birds.

Mommy hugs are full of love.

Daddy hugs are full of love.

There are all kinds of love.

Best Friend love.

Sibling love.

Baby love.

New sibling love.

There's world love.

Everyday is full of love.

Spring love.

Winter love.

Your home is full of love.

Presents are full of love.

A jar full of love. You can fill this jar with anything that brings you love, joy, and happiness.

And here's my love.

In the quiet moments before sleep, little one, always remember — you are a bundle of joy wrapped in love's tender embrace. From the sparkle in your eyes to the warmth of your tiny toes, celebrate the miracle of you. Each giggle, each coo, is a melody of self-love, a symphony of your uniqueness. You are a treasure, a gift to the world, and with every beat of your tiny heart, dance to the rhythm of self-love. Embrace your journey, little one, for you are a masterpiece, and your story is written in the language of love.

Live out loud,
Live to inspire the next generation.

AS PART OF THE "INTERESTING TALES" COLLECTION, "FULL OF LOVE" CONTINUES THE TRADITION OF BRINGING IMAGINATIVE AND CLEVER STORIES TO YOUNG AUDIENCES.

WITH VIBRANT ILLUSTRATIONS AND ENGAGING STORYTELLING, 'FULL OF LOVE' IS NOT JUST A BOOK; IT'S A CELEBRATION OF THE LOVE THAT SURROUNDS CHILDREN EVERY DAY. PERFECT FOR BEDTIME STORIES OR QUIET MOMENTS, THIS ENCHANTING TALE REMINDS BOTH KIDS AND ADULTS ALIKE THAT LOVE IS A MAGICAL FORCE THAT MAKES EVERY DAY EXTRAORDINARY. SHARE THE LOVE AND MAKE 'FULL OF LOVE' A CHERISHED ADDITION TO YOUR FAMILY'S STORYTIME COLLECTION.

OTHER BOOKS BY THIS AUTHOR YOU CAN ENJOY!

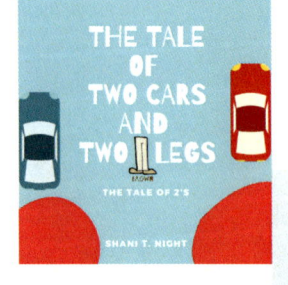

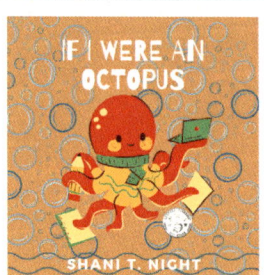

Made in United States
Orlando, FL
22 January 2025

57666907R00024